Please deliver this postcard to:

_____

_____

_____

_____

Visit juniorsread.com

Please deliver this postcard to:

_____

_____

_____

_____

Visit juniorsread.com

Please deliver this postcard to:

_____

_____

_____

_____

Visit juniorsread.com

Please deliver this postcard to:

_____

_____

_____

_____

Visit juniorsread.com

Please deliver this postcard to:

_____

_____

_____

_____

Visit juniorsread.com

Please deliver this postcard to:

_____

_____

_____

Visit juniorsread.com

Annie
Who's ready to soar with me?

Up, up and away! ✈

#blackhistory #blackherstory #inspiration
#siblinglove #pilot #aviation #flying

Share

annie._.izzie

LIVE

Annie
Who are we going to be today?

Izzie
Pick anyone: Simone Manuel @swimone13, Natalie Hinds @_nhinds, Lia Neal @lia_neal.

Annie
We can't go wrong there!

annie._.izzie
We swim because of you. You all inspire us!

Come on, Annie! Let's swim! 🏊

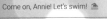

Please deliver this postcard to:

_____

_____

_____

_____

Visit juniorsread.com

Please deliver this postcard to:

_____

_____

_____

_____

Visit juniorsread.com

I ♥ ANNIE & IZZIE

There's no business like show business, sis!

Please deliver this postcard to:

_____

_____

_____

_____

Visit juniorsread.com

Please deliver this postcard to:

_____

_____

_____

_____

Visit juniorsread.com

Ooo Ooo Ooo... 🎤

God bless the child who's got her own!

annie._.izzie

Liked by annie._.izzie and 37 others
annie._.izzie #blackgirlsrock #blackchildren #imblackandimproud #blackexcellence #blackpride #juniorsread #style #blackparents #blackcommunity #blackculture #fencing #womenfencing #sword #swordfighting #squadgoals #fencers #fruits #siblinglove #sisters

Follow @annie._.izzie for new @juniorsread short stories.

Slice, slice, slice ⚔️

Izzie
Apple, mango, watermelon, orange, cherry 🥝🍊🍉🍊🍒🍒

Annie
Slice, slice, slice ⚔️

Izzie
Pineapple, banana, strawberry 🍌🥝🍓

Annie
Slice, slice, slice ⚔️

There has to be an easier way to make fruit salad! ⋮

Please deliver this postcard to:

_____

_____

_____

_____

Visit juniorsread.com

Please deliver this postcard to:

_____

_____

_____

_____

Visit juniorsread.com

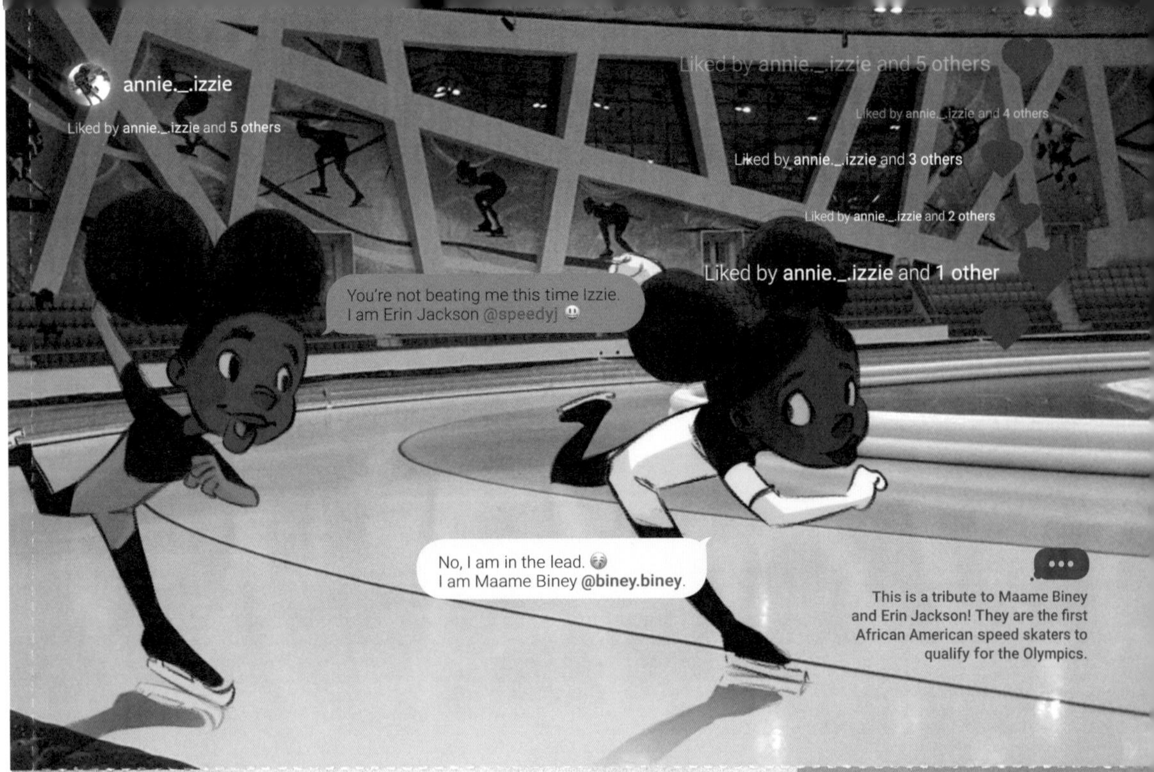

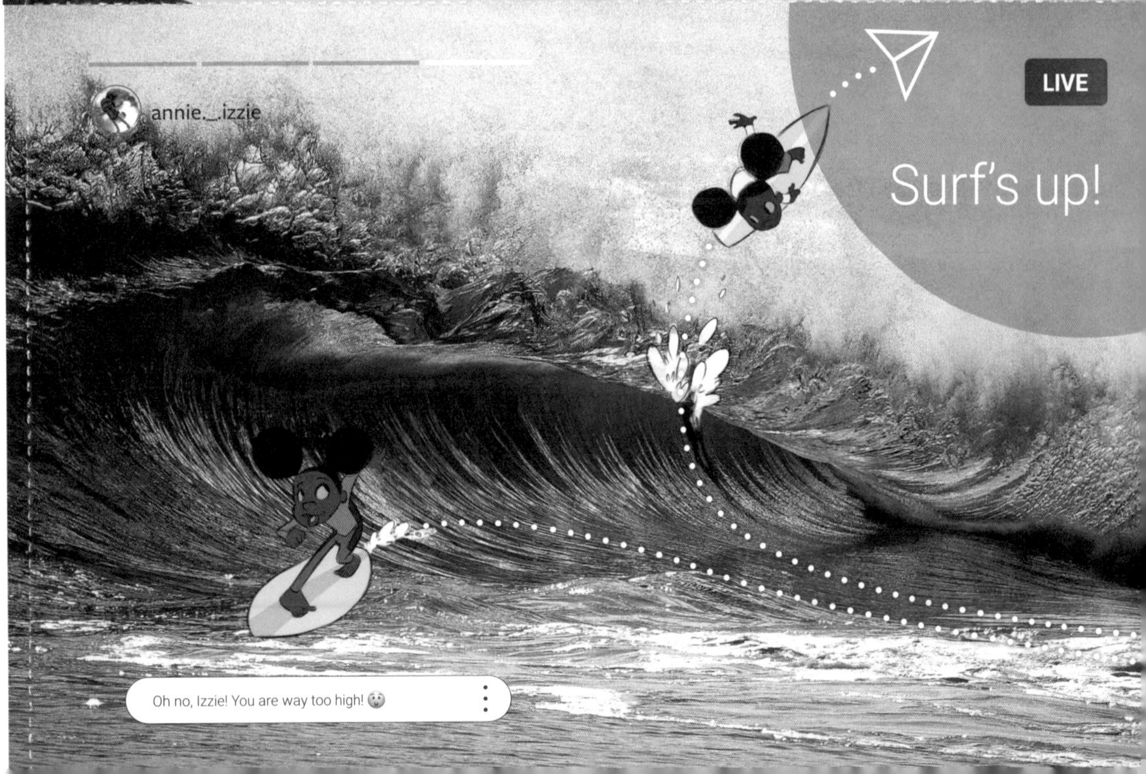

Please deliver this postcard to:

_____

_____

_____

_____

Visit juniorsread.com

Please deliver this postcard to:

_____

_____

_____

_____

Visit juniorsread.com

Please deliver this postcard to:

_____

_____

_____

_____

Visit juniorsread.com

Please deliver this postcard to:

_____

_____

_____

_____

Visit juniorsread.com

Please deliver this postcard to:

_____

_____

_____

_____

Please deliver this postcard to:

_____

_____

_____

_____

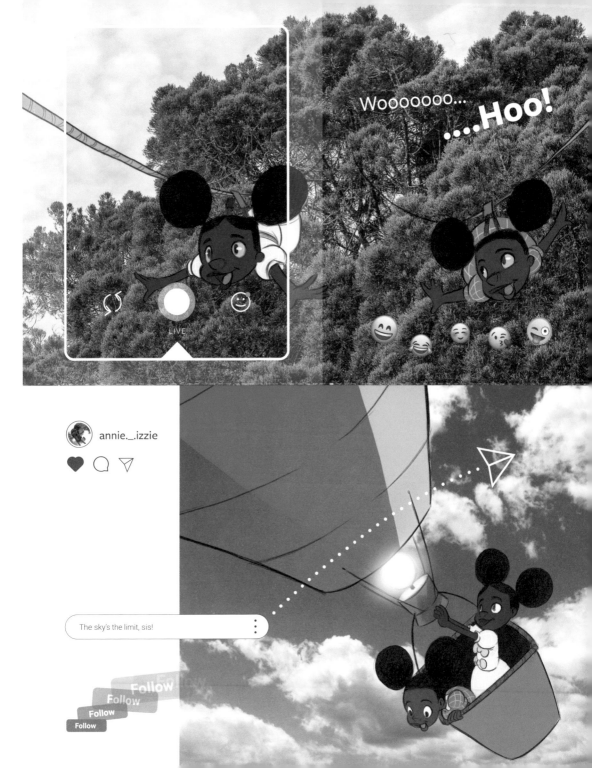

Please deliver this postcard to:

_____

_____

_____

_____

Visit juniorsread.com

Please deliver this postcard to:

_____

_____

_____

_____

Visit juniorsread.com

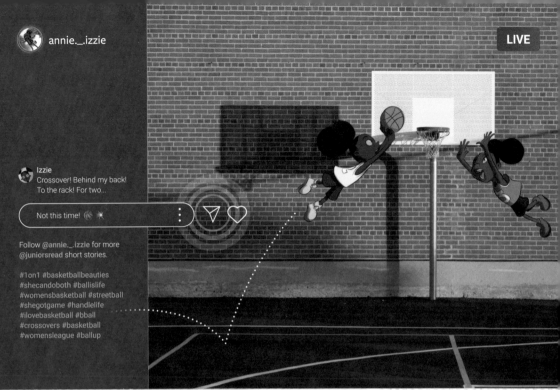

annie._.izzie

LIVE

Izzie
Crossover! Behind my back!
To the rack! For two...

Not this time!

Follow @annie._.izzie for more
@juniorsread short stories.

#1on1 #basketballbeauties
#shecandoboth #ballislife
#womensbasketball #streetball
#shegotgame #handlelife
#ilovebasketball #bball
#crossovers #basketball
#womensleague #ballup

Do you think Mom will like this photo, Annie?

Share

Please deliver this postcard to:

_____

_____

_____

_____

Visit juniorsread.com

Please deliver this postcard to:

_____

_____

_____

_____

Visit juniorsread.com

Please deliver this postcard to:

_____

_____

_____

_____

Visit juniorsread.com

Please deliver this postcard to:

_____

_____

_____

_____

Visit juniorsread.com

Please deliver this postcard to:

_____

_____

_____

_____

Juniors Read

Visit juniorsread.com

Please deliver this postcard to:

_____

_____

_____

_____

Juniors Read

Visit juniorsread.com

Please deliver this postcard to:

_____

_____

_____

_____

Visit juniorsread.com

Please deliver this postcard to:

_____

_____

_____

_____

Visit juniorsread.com

Please deliver this postcard to:

_____

_____

_____

_____

Visit juniorsread.com

Please deliver this postcard to:

_____

_____

_____

_____

Visit juniorsread.com

Please deliver this postcard to:

_____

_____

_____

_____

Visit juniorsread.com

Please deliver this postcard to:

_____

_____

_____

_____

Visit juniorsread.com